SPANKED AT THE ACADEMY

by
Melissa Trump

PUBLISHED BY:
Melissa Trump

'SPANKED AT THE ACADEMY'
Copyright © 2024 by Melissa Trump

No part of this publication may be reproduced
in any form or by any means without
prior permission of the author.
This is a work of fiction. All characters are, and are intended, 18+.

CHAPTER 1

Six is not enough.

Freshman Eugene Hall sat uncomfortably at his desk enduring the withering gaze of his Form Master, Mr Buckmaster. Hall had been engaged in a risky contest of wills with Mr Buckmaster, defying his authority by questioning the new discipline policy that he intended to implement. The policy included restrictions on an offender's liberty as well as corporal punishment. Defiantly, Hall eyeballed his Master which raised his ire further and his face went red with anger. Realising that he had gone too far, Hall lowered his eyes submissively signaling surrender, but this was not enough to save him. He had incurred Mr Buckmaster's displeasure, and he knew that retribution was nigh.

Hall had been a student at the Standfast Academy for about six months, the 24-year-old freshman had formerly served four years in the Army, but a series of disciplinary breaches culminating in him going AWOL had earned him as four-year stint in a Military Correctional Facility. After serving six months of his sentence, he had been paroled on the condition that he completed the two-year Standfast Academy program.

The Standfast Academy is a one-hundred-year-old tertiary education institution founded by Colonel Gordon Standfast VC, MC, who saw a need to provide higher educational opportunities for young men who had no formal education but who had showed promise in pursuits like soldiering or other challenging life experiences. Students were individualistic, tough young fellows who harboured a healthy cynicism towards authority and liked to challenge it whenever the opportunity arose. Accordingly, academic life at the Academy was imbued with a tough military ethos founded on the principle of strict discipline in which corporal punishment, and forced nudity, played a large part.

The Academy motto: wisdom through discipline, successfully encapsulates its essence.

Today, in academic circles, the Academy is regarded as an anachronism but resolute Masters, a loyal alumni and committed students have ensured that the Academy's ethos has survived the passing years and remained true to its founder's beliefs and character.

Mr Buckmaster was new to the Academy, he had intended his tenure to be short before moving on, but he quickly come to believe in the Academy's mission and saw that he had a role to play in carrying it out. He was a physically big, thick set man who had been a keen boxer in his university days. His large physical presence, a no-nonsense approach to classroom discipline and a keen sense of dedication to his role as an educator of young men gave him a commanding presence in the classroom.

Mr Buckmaster handed Hall a copy of the Academy's discipline regulations.

"Show me where it says that I can't award a student corporal punishment and a restriction of liberty, Hall," he said.

Hall replied that he had not read the regulations. "But it is common knowledge and practice that dual punishment awards are not allowed, Sir," he argued.

Mr Buckmaster glared at the young man sitting in front of him.

"If you bothered to read the regulations Hall, you would know that they grant me a large degree of discretion when it comes to awarding punishments," he snapped. "And that does not include just corporal punishment."

Hall hung his head in silence, but he remained obdurate.

"Well Hall, what have you got to say for yourself?" he demanded. Hall remained silent.

Mr Buckmaster had had enough of Hall and his insolence.

"Dumb insolence!" he roared. "You need a lesson young man, approach the front," he ordered.

Hall reluctantly stood up and walked to the front of the

classroom, stopping in front of a desk that served as a punishment bench.

Mr Buckmaster considered Hall's punishment, he knew that a lad like Hall was a lusty young man who had acquired some life experience, and it would require a sound thrashing to gain his attention. The standard schoolroom *six of the best* would not suffice, but a dozen strokes delivered across his bare bottom would do the job.

Awarding punishment, Mr Buckmaster said: "You are to receive twelve strokes of the discipline paddle across your bare bottom, and you are restricted to the Academy precinct next Saturday."

Hall needed to show his classmates that Mr Buckmaster did not intimidate him. "Yes Sir, thank you Sir," he called out in a confident voice, a voice that disguised the butterflies in his stomach.

"Prepare yourself, Hall. Remove your blazer and trousers," Mr Buckmaster said.

"Excuse me, sir?"

"If you had cared to read the regulation, you would know that punishment are always given in the nude. This is because we firmly believe that forced nudity strengthens the message we want to give."

Hall reluctantly obeyed removing his blazer, shoes and trousers and folding them neatly on Mr Buckmaster's desk.

"Probably I didn't speak clearly, young Mr Hall," Mr Buckmaster said. "Naked means naked. Remove the remaining items of clothing you are wearing, socks too."

"But… in front of the whole class?"

"Yes, Mr Hall. That's exactly what public nudity means. Stop being shy, you have seen your fellow students naked under the showers, and so have they. You will be punished naked. And you will scream and kick about naked. This will help your attitude."

Hall obeyed. He bent to remove his socks, and he was happy that he hadn't removed his underwear before, since it would have exposed his anus to his peers view.

"Now stay in position and show yourself to the class, while I prepare."

Hall placed his hands on his head and stood in front of the bench keeping his eye to his front, as was the practice at the Academy, standing totally exposed to his peers.

Zachary Dillon, who was Hall's best friend watched with dismay and concern at his friend's predicament. He has dug himself into a big hole, he thought.

For his part Mr Buckmaster had learnt enough about Hall to know that he was a bright young man who harboured a bolshie attitude. He clearly needed a good lesson. He opened a tall cupboard in the corner of the classroom and rummaged through a collection of canes and leather straps, slowly, so to keep him naked as long as possible, still and silent in front of the whole class, until he found the class discipline paddle. The paddle was constructed from a solid piece of Jarrah timber and was about two inches thick, five inches wide and two feet long including the wooden handle. The paddle had two rows of holes drilled at close intervals along its blade. The rich reddish-brown heartwood of the Jarrah provided a hard, even surface. He loved the way that tool worked on young, unblemished skin.

Mr Buckmaster clutched the paddle in his big right fist. "Bend over, Hall," he ordered.

Hall reluctantly stretched his slim frame across the bench, and reaching forward, he grasped the rail at the back.

"Bend right over, tighten your bottom," Mr Buckmaster said. "I promise this will hurt."

Hall obeyed by wriggling further over the bench and raising his bottom high, exposing his well-rounded, manly orbs. Mr Buckmaster positioned himself to Hall's left so that his paddle and outstretched arm were at right angles to Hall's orbs. He tapped Hall's bottom twice with his paddle. "It is a dozen for you, young man," he said.

"Yes Sir!" Hall replied. He tried to sound normal, but his voice quavered.

There was complete silence in the classroom as every eye focused on Hall's beautifully presented bottom. Lads at the back of the classroom had to reposition themselves to get a clear view of the impending action. A heady atmosphere of homoeroticism hung in the air as their excitement mounted, and many of them, thought trying to conceal this, had raging boners.

Mr Buckmaster swung the paddle back as far as he could then violently swung it forward, it landed across Hall's waiting bottom with a sharp CRACK.

"OH!" Hall gasped as he absorbed the shock of the first stroke. Hall had been around classrooms long enough to know that the first stroke always hurts more than expected.

"That's good. Keep on screaming, and cry if you have too," Mr Buckmaster said. "The goal of humiliation is to make you a better person."

CRACK the second stroke made him gasp louder and he rocked his body back and forth trying to alleviate the sting.

"Keep still, Hall," Mr Buckmaster commanded. "Or I'll have to start again."

"Oh, yes Sir," Hall moaned.

Mr Buckmaster slowly meted out the swats allowing time for the effect of each impact to fully develop before he delivered the next full impact blow. Hall's gasps grew louder as the sting built up across his smarting bottom and he lifted his legs and writhed on the bench in an effort to alleviate his suffering. Hall tried not to blub in front of Mr Buckmaster and his classmates, but tears soon filled his eyes.

Hall's classmates were transfixed by the unfolding spectacle. They silently counted off the strokes and watched as a bright red hue built up around his exposed bottom. Their enjoyment was not personal. They knew that they were all eligible for this treatment, and be asked to strip totally naked to be thrashed in front of the others. But they were turned on by the imposition of Academy discipline and the personal interaction between the authoritarian Master and submissive student.

Finally, Hall's ordeal by paddle was over and he was told to stand up still totally naked, and ask the class to excuse him for having interrupted their education. Then he was allowed to dress himself. He tried desperately to alleviate the pain by rubbing his bottom and he turned away from his classmates while he dressed so that they could not see his red face and hot tears of shame and pain. Mr Buckmaster reminded Hall that, as an additional punishment, he was grounded next Saturday.

"Yes Sir," Hall replied submissively. He had lost his bad attitude.

On his way out at the end of the class, Mr Buckmaster called Hall over and, holding out his hand, he said: "No hard feelings, Hall."

Hall took his hand and replied: "No Sir. Thanks for the lesson Sir."

Zac was waiting for him outside the classroom. He gave Eugene a big hug and tousled his hair.

"Who has been a naughty boy?" he teased.

"Leave me alone, Zac. My bum hurts like hell," he said.

"You looked good, believe me, and took it like the man you are. Sure, I will leave you alone – for now. But tonight, after lights out I am going to give you what you really need," he said grinning wickedly.

Eugene smiled back.

CHAPTER 2

A visit to the headmaster's office

It was a busy Sunday afternoon at the Academy. The staff were all in attendance to welcome the students returning from their autumn leave and prepare for the coming term. Miss Price, the headmaster's assistant was at work at her desk in the outer office. Freshman Eugene Hall entered the office clutching a piece of paper. She looked up and smiled. She liked Hall. He was a gentle young man who was always polite and respectful to her. His behaviour differed from other students who openly lusted after her and tried to *chat her up*.

"Hello, Eugene, how was your leave?" she asked.

"It was ok until today, Miss. I think I need to see the headmaster," he said with a long face. He gave her the paper that he was holding. It was an on-the-spot fine of $200 issued by a transit authority officer for drinking alcohol on the train.

"Oh, Eugene. Yes you do need to see the headmaster. Do you have clean underpants?" she said.

"Miss. Please."

"I'm sorry, I just hope it is. He gets really angry when he sees a lack of hygiene during the punishments. Yesterday he didn't allow Green to dress again after his thrashing. Poor man had to get back to the classroom naked as he was, and had to stay naked in class the whole day. I wonder if this thing, even though effective as it is, is getting out of hand. But it does have a good effect on you, I'm afraid to say." Hitting the intercom button she said, "Sir, Freshman Hall is here to see you."

"Ask him to wait," Doctor Barton, the headmaster replied. Miss Price knew how her boss worked. There were more than two hundred students at the Academy, and he needed to check Hall's personal information, his academic results, and his disciplinary record before he saw him. Doctor Barton was a thorough man and Hall waited anxiously for about ten minutes before he was called into his office. At least, this time he hadn't have him strip naked before entering.

Hall had time to reflect on his situation. He relied on his grandparents, who owned a small farm, for financial support. His grandfather provided him with a small monthly allowance, but he was always short of money, so he was unable to pay the $200 fine.

When he entered the headmaster's office the memories flooded back. The last time he was in this room was when he came before the Academy selection board to determine his suitability for enrolment. His parole from the military correctional establishment was contingent upon him being accepted by the Academy. That time he had been escorted, in handcuffs, by a prison officer. He was shabbily dressed and sported a black eye; it was not a good first impression and he failed to convince the board. It was only Doctor Barton's intervention that saved him from being rejected and sent back to prison. Hall felt ashamed that now, just months later, he had let him down through his stupidity.

Doctor Barton sat at his desk he was a sophisticated, 50-year-old man who carried with him an air of authority that a lifetime of success had bestowed upon him. He was always immaculately dressed from his starched collar to the high shine on his shoes. Physically robust he commanded respect from his students. Standing opposite him, Hall felt like a grubby little grommet who wore the same underpants all week.

The headmaster greeted Hall in a friendly fashion, "Welcome back Hall, how was your leave?"

Hall wanted to delay the unwelcome news, he replied: "Um, good. Thank you, Sir."

"What did you do with yourself?" he asked.

Hall told him that he had spent the time helping his grandpa repair the fences on the farm.

"Ah, a working holiday!" He exclaimed. "That's very healthy.

Hard working and sweating bare-chested under the sun. Let me see your hands Hall," he added.

Hall showed him his bruised and battered hands. "Ah yes, the hands of a working man. Nothing to be ashamed of," he said looking kindly at Hall. "What can I do for you young man?" the headmaster finally asked.

Hall handed him the citation from the transit authority. "I copped a $200 fine for drinking beer on the train, Sir," he said.

The headmaster frowned and his demeanour changed. He read the citation carefully. This was not the first time that he had seen a citation from a transit authority officer. Several of his students had received one, often for the most specious of reasons. The same officer had issued them. "Tell me what happened Hall," he said.

Hall explained that he had fallen in with a group of shearers who were travelling to the high country for work. They were having a few beers and they had asked him to join them. "It was a hot day, Sir, so the beer went down well, but we were all busted, cans in hand, by a transit authority officer," he said.

The headmaster asked, "Have you been issued with a citation from a transit authority officer before, Hall?"

"No Sir, this is the first time," Hall said.

The headmaster called Miss Price into his office; he handed her the citation. "Miss Price, Hall received this today it is his first offence, he should receive a warning, not a fine. Please check this out with your contact in the transit authority office."

"With pleasure, Sir," Miss Price replied. She gave Hall a conspiratorial wink.

"I like to follow procedures, Mr Hall. That should take care of the fine, but it still leaves the issues that you broke the law and worse, you broke it when you were off campus in your Academy uniform," the headmaster said.

Hall was very apologetic, "I am deeply sorry Sir, especially after what you have done for me. I have let you down. You should thrash me, Sir, very severely" Hall said. "I don't know why I do this stuff, Sir," he added.

The headmaster nodded. "It is not the crime of Century, Hall, but there must be consequences." He then gave Hall his punishment: "You are to receive twelve strokes of the strap, six across your underpants and six on your bare bottom, Hall," he said. "And you are grounded next weekend," he added.

"Yes Sir, thank you, Sir," Hall replied. He thought he had got off lightly; however, he had yet to suffer a thrashing from the headmaster, and he soon discovered that he was not getting off lightly.

Hall was conscious of the infringements he had racked up during his time at the Academy and the spankings he had received for them. "With my disciplinary record, I am concerned that you may send me back to prison, Sir," Hall said nervously.

The headmaster shook his head and said. "No Hall, our job is to educate you, teach you discipline and keep you out of prison. Your job is to study hard, be honest about your mistakes and take what is coming to you. Getting your bottom smacked is part of that – it is the Academy way."

Hall looked his headmaster in the eye and said: "Thank you, Sir."

"Well, you know the procedure. So please begin."

"All my clothes, Sir?"

"Yes Hall," the headmaster replied.

Hall started with his shoes and socks, getting the usual weird feeling of being barefoot on the hard wooden floor. But that was just the beginning. Soon he was bare-chested.

"The tan look good on your young body."

"Thank you, Sir."

Hall removed all his clothes except for his white underpants and military dog tags. He wore his dog tags as a lucky talisman. The headmaster removed his own jacket and his tie and rolled up his right shirt sleeve. He then rummaged around in a cupboard looking for his strap. Then he remembered that he had left it in the outer office after he had thrashed all the members of the Academy rugby team for the fight that they started after the grand final match at the end of last term.

He told Hall to go next door and fetch the strap. "Dressed like this, Sir?" he asked.

"No, now that you have asked. I said you would receive six strokes on the bare and six on the pants, but I didn't say in which order. You have to learn to ask no questions when you are punished, one day this may save your life, or your career. You will fetch it naked, so take off your pants, please. You will wear them again after the first six strokes."

Hall was a bit bewildered at this change of plans, but knew better than to ask another question. The Headmaster could be a caring man when concerned with the future of his students, but he knew he had to be strict just because of that.

"Hall, hurry up. I haven't got all day," he said.

"Sorry, Sir. Yes, Sir." Hall put his thumbs in the elastic band of his underpants and drew them down his legs, stepping out of them and giving them to the Headmaster like the rest of his clothes. He didn't cover his nakedness. He knew this would have earned him two more strokes.

Blushing, barefoot, totally naked, Hall went to the outer office and said: "Sorry for my appearance in this state, Miss Price. I am looking for the headmaster's strap."

Miss Price's eyes widened at the sight of Hall wearing only his dog tags on his beautiful, tanned chest. He was a slightly built, but well-muscled lad with a washboard stomach, and his penis… she obviously tried not to look at the long tool Hall had between his legs, which made him proud, somehow, every time he had to strip naked for punishment.

She retrieved the strap from a drawer, cleared her throat, and handed it to him. "Sorry, Eugene. I forgot to put it back in Doctor Barton's office after he used it to punish the rugby team," she said.

Hall held the strap in both hands. He was surprised how heavy it felt. He got back in, showing all the glory of his backside to Miss Price, and handed the strap to the headmaster; it was a prison strap about two feet long and four inches wide. It had seen a lot of service correcting the behaviour of young Academy men, the leather was scuffed and faded, but it was still a potent instrument of punishment.

The headmaster told Hall to bend over the front of his desk. Hall lay across the desk, and reaching forward, he grasped the edge at the back. "Spread your legs and raise your bottom, Hall," he said.

Hall obeyed.

The headmaster grunted his satisfaction at the sight of Hall's well-presented bottom. His two well-rounded orbs and his crack were clearly defined.

"Six on the bare, then your underpants, Hall," the headmaster said.

"Yes Sir," Hall replied.

The headmaster believed that discipline was best served by delivering a bruising thrashing that the punishment lad would long remember. He swung the strap back as far as he could and then whipped it forward, it landed across Hall's waiting bottom with a sharp Thwap.

"Ouch!" Hall cried out as he absorbed its bruising sting.

He allowed time for Hall to absorb the strap's punitive effect before laying on the next stroke.

Thwap

"Ouch, Ouch!" Hall cried out again. In her outer office, Miss Price could hear the strap as it cracked across Hall's bare bottom and his cries. She grimaced. She knew that the punishment was justified and necessary, but she felt sorry for Hall. He is a gentle boy, not a lot like most of the toughs, she thought. But she felt excited somehow, and couldn't deny herself. She looked around. She was alone. She took a hand to her slit, and massaged herself as the erotic sounds of the punishment next door reached her ears.

The headmaster slowly meted out the next four swats, Hall's cries grew louder as the pain built up across his naked bottom. If he could have seen his bottom he would have noticed the red hue developing around the exposed parts of his buttocks.

As Hall's anxiety built up, sweat started to glisten on his skin and, as it flowed, the tangy scent of Hall's body odour developed adding to the testosterone-charged, masochistic atmosphere that pervaded the headmaster's office.

It was time to help him dress again before the final six strokes.

The headmaster stared at Hall's white underpants on his desk.

He noticed the inscription around the band, Military Correctional Establishment. "Where did you get those underpants, Hall?" he asked.

"They are prison issues, Sir," Hall replied. Hall liked wearing his gaol house underpants. They were his lucky undies.

"I'm sorry but I can't allow you to wear them during a punishment," the headmaster said.

"Yes Sir," Hall replied. "I understand. I accept to receive the remaining six strokes still in the nude. It will help me correct my attitude."

"That it will."

Hall's bottom was covered in black and blue bruises.

"Bend over again Hall. It's another six on your bare bottom," the headmaster said.

Hall had received the strap from the Jesuit fathers when he was at school, but the strapping that he was receiving from the headmaster felt much more painful.

He bent over and without being told spread his legs and raised his bottom.

The headmaster stared at Hall's nether region, his genitals and bottom were hairless. "Why are you shaved Hall?" he asked.

Hall blushed. He was about to tell his headmaster the truth – that his boyfriend had told him to shave, but he changed his mind and said: "Um, it's a cultural practice in prison, Sir. I find it more hygienic."

The headmaster was sceptical, but he decided not to pursue this line of investigation.

"Maintain that position, Hall," he said. "I will try to make them more painful, to help you."

"Yes Sir," Hall replied. "I understand it is for my good."

The headmaster proceeded to award Hall the final six strokes of the strap. Hall's backside was beaten black and blue, it throbbed, and he wriggled his body and crossed his legs to try and alleviate the intense pain. He cried out loudly as the Headmaster slowly meted out each excruciating stroke. Tears filled his eyes and flowed down his face, he wanted to beg him to stop but he didn't want his headmaster to think that he couldn't take his thrashing.

Finally, it was over. He was told to stand. He grabbed his throbbing butt cheeks with his hands and rubbed them vigorously while simultaneously tapping out a dance on the floor. His manhood flopped up and down unashamedly, and the tears flowed freely as he sobbed. He didn't feel embarrassed that his headmaster saw him this way, the pain was all-consuming.

The headmaster told him to face the wall and allowed him time to recover his composure. Hall stood facing the wall for some time with his legs apart and his hands on his head, slowly the intensity of the pain abated, and he stopped sobbing. As the heat covering his bottom slowly spread between his legs, Hall's manhood stirred. The headmaster felt a pang of guilt, he had misjudged his tolerance to pain.

"Are you ok, Hall," he asked.

"Yes Sir," Hall sniffed.

He told Hall to get dressed. "You took that well, Hall," he said.

Hall wiped the tears from his face with the back of his hand, he said: "Thank you, Sir. That was the hardest thrashing that I have ever received."

Hall was recovering his mojo, as he dressed he caught his headmaster's eye and allowed him a glimpse of his throbbing erection before quickly burying it in his pants.

The headmaster grinned knowingly.

Fully dressed Hall stood in front of the headmaster and gently rubbed the bruises on his bottom.

"Is there any other bad news that you wish to declare Hall?" the headmaster asked.

"No Sir, that's all for now. It was good to spend quality time with you, Sir," he said.

Doctor Barton tried not to smile as he waved his finger at the cheeky young man. "I am sure that you will provide the opportunity for us to get together again Hall," he said. "There may be some more instruments of procedures I'd like to try."

"Like what, Sir?"

"I've recently read about a typical oriental spanking procedure, which focuses on feet alone."

"That sounds painful, Sir. It could make it hard to walk, after the punishment."

"Yes, Hall. That's probably the aim of that. Now get out of my sight."

Hall grinned.

Hall walked awkwardly out of the office with his hands clasped firmly on his butt cheeks. He realised that he had just undergone a rite of passage – his first disciplinary visit to the headmaster's office.

CHAPTER 3

A birthday ponding

Freshman Eugene Hall was feeling anxious. There was mischief brewing in the dorm and he knew that he was going to be the butt of it. Today was his 24th birthday and it was a tradition at the Academy to subject a birthday boy to a *ponding*. That meant being stripped naked by his classmates and unceremoniously dumped into the fetid waters of the Academy fountain. It was a tradition that was not supported by the Academy staff it was a punishable offense, which is why it was conducted as clandestinely as possible.

Suddenly the door to his room burst open and his best mate Zac Dillon and three other lusty lads descended upon him. They unceremoniously stripped him of his clothing, Zac grabbed the seam on his underpants intent on ripping them apart. "NO!" Eugene cried. "It is my last pair." But he was too late. There was a loud ripping sound as his undies were ripped asunder and his penis flopped around. The boys grabbed his arms and his legs and, in the company of the rest of his classmates, he was carted protesting outside. It was a cold and dark night and. Anxious to get back inside, they quickly carried him towards the pond. Suddenly a torch flashed, and a voice challenged them. "Halt, who goes there?"

"Fuck, it is one of the porters," somebody whispered.

"Stay where you are," the porter commanded.

They had almost reached the edge of the pond. "Ok boys, that's close enough, toss him in," Zac said. They swung him back and forth like a sack of potatoes and then released him.

Eugene flew and splashed into the pond. He cried out as the right side of his body was grazed on its jagged inside surface. Except for Zac, the boys scarpered back to their dorm narrowly escaping the arrival of the porter.

Zac helped Eugene climb out of the pond. He could see that he was grazed and bleeding.

"Names?" Mr Graham, the night porter, demanded. They sheepishly gave him their names. "What about the others, what are their names?" Mr Graham asked. Zac knew that he could not rat on his mates, it was part of the Academy ethos.

Zac shook his head. "I don't know Sir," he replied.

"Right, you two are on report for this and it will attract consequences. I will mention in my report that you refused to divulge the names of your accomplices," he said.

The boys nodded their heads in acceptance. "Yes Sir," Zac replied.

Eugene spent an uncomfortable night nursing his injuries, and first thing the next morning, Zac escorted him to the Academy clinic. The medical orderly, Mr Triage, examined him.

"Let me guess, a botched ponding," he said.

"Yes Sir," Zac replied.

"Are you responsible for this, Dillon?" he asked.

"Yes Sir, I wanted Eugene to have a memorable birthday," he replied. He regretted what he had done.

Eugene stood naked while Mr Triage patched him up.

Instead of the furtive glances that he and Eugene exchanged while naked in the shower, Zac was able to observe his friend's naked form openly and closely. Eugene was a slightly built, well-proportioned young man, reminiscent of Michelangelo's iconic statue of David. Zac's manhood stirred.

Mr Triage told Eugene that the pond was full of nasty bugs and that he needed a tetanus shot. He produced a syringe and told him to bend over the treatment bench. "It is best if you get it in your butt, Hall," he said. Zac grinned at the look of alarm that crossed his friend's face.

"Which cheek do you want it in Hall?" Mr Triage asked.

"Um, the left. No, the right. Um, you choose Sir," he stammered.

Ok, the left cheek, Mr Triage said as he tapped the crown

of Eugene's left butt cheek with two fingers. "Relax, Hall. Don't clench your butt," he said. He threw the needle like a dart into Eugene's well-rounded orb.

"Ouch!" Eugene cried.

"Now, a little prick," Mr Triage said as he emptied the contents of the syringe into his muscle.

"Oww, Ouch!" he cried again. "That is more than just a little prick," he complained.

Mr Triage grinned and said, "You boys, you will laugh when you break your arm on the footy field but cry when you receive a little needle."

"That's ok for you to say, Sir. You didn't get it," Hall retorted.

Mr Triage put a band-aid over the needle site and gave his butt a tap with his hand. "Try to stay out of trouble for a few days, Hall," he said.

"We are already in trouble. We are both on report, Sir," Zac told him.

"Good, then you will get what is coming to you, Dillon," Mr Triage said.

Mr Triage gave Hall light duties for six days and wrote upon the form that, because of extensive grazing and bruising around his right buttock, he recommended that he not be spanked until his injuries had recovered.

"Can I have one of those too, Sir?" Zac asked.

"No, you can't," Mr Triage replied. "And stand to attention Dillon," he ordered.

Zac came to attention and Mr Triage reprimanded him for the ponding and the unsafe way it was conducted. "This is what happens when you break the rules. You are a former soldier, Dillon, you should have more sense."

"Sir. No excuse, Sir," Zac replied.

They both felt chastened as they made their way to class. They knew that their Form Master, Mr Buckmaster, would have received Mr Graham's report by now and that punishment loomed.

"You two are late," Mr Buckmaster, said.

He had read, with rising anger, the report from Mr Graham

about the ponding incident and he resolved to inflict stern punishments on all the lads involved. Even by Academy standards, Mr Buckmaster had a reputation for being a stern disciplinarian.

Eugene handed Mr Buckmaster his light duties note. He read it and declared: "I decide your punishment, not the medical staff, Hall."

Eugene had learned the hard way not to butt heads with Mr Buckmaster. "Yes, Sir," he replied.

Mr Buckmaster turned to the first order of business, the report from Mr Graham. "It says here that you two were caught engaging in a ponding, an activity that is banned. What say you?" he asked. There was silence. "Well Hall, speak up."

"Guilty as charged, Sir," Eugene replied.

"Sir, Hall was the victim of the ponding. It was my fault," Zac said.

"The rules are quite clear. With these illicit activities, all participants are guilty. The Academy takes this sort of risky behavior very seriously and there must be consequences for all involved," Mr Buckmaster said. Looking sternly at Hall and Dillon he said: "I will begin with you two." Eugene noticed that the cane, a medium-thickness rattan with a hooked handle, lay waiting on Mr Buckmaster's desk.

"You first Hall, you are to receive six strokes of the cane across your hands," Mr Buckmaster said. "But of course you won't be exempted from complete nudity during punishment just because I'm not hitting any commonly unexposed part."

Eugene blanched; he hated getting the cane across his hands. He much preferred getting it across his bottom. "May I receive it on my bottom Sir?" he asked.

"If it was up to me Hall, you would get it across your bottom naked in the courtyard, that's where you deserve it. But Mr Triage has provided me with a medical recommendation and I must comply with it," Mr Buckmaster said. "Now. Out of your clothes, turn, and face the class. And hold out your right hand," Mr Buckmaster instructed.

Eugene stripped totally naked under everyone's stare, as always starting with shoes and socks, since naked meant naked. In the end of the fast process, he drew down his underpants, and as always he quite proudly showed his long penis.

He held his hand out tucking his thumb under his forefinger to prevent it from taking the full force of the blow. Mr Buckmaster picked up the cane and positioned himself so that he stood a cane's length from Eugene's outstretched hand. He raised the cane high and brought it down forcefully. The cane scythed through the air with a loud thwip. "Oh!" Eugene cried out as it cracked across the palm of his hand. The pain was excruciating, and he dropped his hand and rubbed it on his thigh.

"Put your hand back into position, Hall!" Mr Buckmaster snapped.

Eugene reluctantly lifted his hand, it was shaking.

Mr Buckmaster landed another forceful stroke, with such a force that his penis dangled forward and back.

"Oh!" Eugene cried out as he absorbed the impact of the second stroke. He dropped his hand again. He forced himself to lift it back, but it was shaking badly.

"Take your punishment like a man, Hall," Mr Buckmaster said.

"Yes Sir. Sorry Sir." Stung by this remark, Eugene pulled himself together, changed his position, and supported his hand by placing his left hand underneath it. It held steady.

Mr Buckmaster raised his cane again and brought it down hard across Eugene's throbbing right hand.

He cried again as he took the stroke. His hand shook as the sting built up, but he quickly steadied it and waited for the next stinging cut. The problem was, that the pain and the humiliation as always had a certain kind of effect on him, and his penis started to swell under everyone's astonished stare. Everybody knew that could be a common reaction to a public punishment, and pretended not to see, even though it generally caught most of the attention.

"Change hands," Mr Buckmaster ordered.

Eugene presented his left hand for punishment and managed to take the next three swinging strokes stoically, although he cried out loudly upon receiving each cut. Of course, every time he was hit, his penis swelled even more, and soon it was standing proudly, purple head showing, straight, hard, and somehow beautiful with its perfect veins and proportions above the dangling balls.

His ordeal was over, he was told to take his seat.

"Can I get my clothes back?"

"No. As an additional punishment you will attend this lesson naked. No hard feelings, Hall. You may get your clothes back when you leave," Mr Buckmaster said.

"No Sir, it's discipline, Sir," he replied. "Thank you."

Eugene thrust his hands underneath his armpits, knowing that covering one's genitals was forbidden during the periods of public exposure. He was sweating from the stress of his ordeal. He took his seat hoping that his classmates didn't notice his red face and watery eyes. His classmates, who had watched intently as he took his caning, did notice but they took no joy in watching him suffer, but some took a lot of joy in watching his still hard, straight penis.

Mr Buckmaster turned his attention to Zac. "Dillon. You were the instigator of the ponding, and you deserve the harshest punishment," he said.

"Yes Sir. No excuse Sir," he replied.

Passing sentence Mr Buckmaster said: "You are to receive twelve strokes of the cane across your bare bottom. Prepare yourself, young man."

"Yes Sir," Zac replied.

Zac removed his blazer, shoes, socks, and trousers and stowed them neatly on a chair. Then came his shirt and vests, but not his underpants.

Mr Buckmaster pointed his cane at a spot on the raised teacher's platform at the front of the classroom, and said: "Stand there Dillon. Assume the position and apologize to the class." Zac obeyed and placed his hands on his head. He held his head high, and said. "I want to apologize for disrupting your education with the public showing of my punishment. I hope this will be a useful example for you, to help you avoid stupid attitudes and behaviors."

Just when he finished saying this, Mr Buckmaster drew his

thumbs inside the elastic bands of Zac's underwear and rapidly drew them down his long, athletic legs, raising one of the lad's foot to remove the garment, then the other, before having him wear the pants on his head as an additional humiliation.

"Bend over," Mr Buckmaster said.

"Yes Sir," Zac said.

Wanting to get his ordeal underway, Zac quickly bent over. He was a well-proportioned young man and, while keeping his legs straight, he could bend right over and touch the top of his feet. He felt Mr Buckmaster's hand on his lower back for steadiness. Mr Buckmaster and the lads in the class gazed approvingly at Zac's well presented bottom. His well-rounded orbs were divided by a luxuriant blush of black hair that expanded between his legs. His impressive manhood hung arrogantly between his muscular thighs.

Mr Buckmaster prepared for his exertions by removing his jacket, loosening his tie, and rolling up the sleeve on his right arm. He selected a spot below the top of Zac's buttocks and tapped it with his cane. He then delivered a full-strength stroke across that spot. His cane scythed through the air with a loud thwip and landed across his bottom with a sharp thwap. The sound of the impact of Master's cane on lad's hide reverberated around the classroom and could be heard outside in the hallway. Zac grunted as he felt the cane's agonizing sting. A straight white line immediately appeared across Zac's bottom, which slowly turned pink and then red as it developed into a throbbing, red welt.

Mr Buckmaster allowed about 20 seconds to elapse, time for Zac to fully absorb and appreciate the punitive effects of the stroke before he delivered the next. Again, Zac grunted as he felt its sting and another welt appeared on his bottom, parallel and slightly below the first. Mr Buckmaster was an expert caner, and he laid each successive stroke lower and parallel to the one above. The pain was excruciating and sweat started to dampen Zac's skin and soak through his shirt. However, he managed to hold his position without correction and take each stroke almost silently.

Mr Buckmaster was also sweating from his exertions as he

delivered the twelve blistering strokes across Zac's deserving bottom. The last stroke was delivered across his sensitive *sit spot* where his buttocks joined his thighs. It took him over 4 minutes to deliver Zac's thrashing.

After Mr Buckmaster had delivered the last stroke, without being told, Zac stood up. "I didn't give you permission to stand, Dillon. Bend over again!" Mr Buckmaster snapped, and Zac bent over immediately. "That will cost you an extra stroke."

"Yes, Sir," Zac replied.

Mr Buckmaster decided that Dillon still had some cockiness left in him and that needed to undergo more suffering. He delivered the extra stroke across the back of his thighs, knowing that the welt would be visible when wearing his shorts in gym classes. "Stay in that position Dillon," he said.

"Yes Sir," Zac replied as he fought the urge to stand up and rub his smarting bottom.

Zac remained bent over. Due to his elevated position on the teacher's platform, his classmates got an unobstructed view of his swollen bottom and the red horizontal stripes covering it. The masochistic nature of Zac's thrashing and the sight of his well-punished bottom caused some to shift uncomfortably in their chairs as they tried to accommodate their stirring manhoods.

Mr Buckmaster turned to the last item of business. Looking around the room, he asked: "Who else besides Dillon and Hall participated in the ponding?" There was a resentful silence as the lads avoided eye contact with him. "Oh, come on, you are not schoolboys any more. You are young men. Real men fess up and pay up," he scolded. The silence continued until finally Freshman James, the class captain, stood up and said: "It was all of us Sir, we all participated."

"Just as I thought," Mr Buckmaster said. "As punishment, the whole class is restricted to the campus for the weekend." He waited for the usual excuses and sob stories.

James spoke up again. "Excuse me, Sir. But we are having Hall's birthday party tonight and we have booked and paid a deposit at the bowling alley. I request that we be allowed to complete that activity before we commence our period of restrictions."

Mr Buckmaster was about to give his usual too bad so sad response to requests like this, but he reconsidered. "Alright, James. The period of your restrictions will start at 23:00 hours tonight. Be back on campus by then, I will be checking."

"Thank you, Sir," James replied.

Mr Buckmaster told Zac, who was still in the punishment position, to stand and get back to his seat; naked, of course, just like Eugene. Zac stood awkwardly, the side effects of his thrashing had given him a boner. Mr Buckmaster's eyes widened as he caught a glimpse of Zac's huge boner curving arrogantly upwards.

Mr Buckmaster held out his hand and asked: "No hard feelings, Dillon?"

Taking the outstretched hand, Zac gave him a lopsided grin. "No Sir, I had it coming."

Through the classroom window, Mr Buckmaster watched as Eugene and Zac left for the afternoon, once again clothed. Eugene walked awkwardly nursing his bruises and Zac did his best to walk normally and not rub his smarting posterior or skip. Mr Buckmaster smiled, even though they felt sore and sorry for themselves today, he knew that in years to come both young men would look back on Hall's birthday ponding nostalgically.

CHAPTER 4

The relief master

It was the usual busy Saturday morning at the Burger Treat restaurant, the favourite eating haunt for Standfast Academy students. The restaurant was full of casually attired raucous young men paying each other out and shouting at each other across the room. In contrast to the noisy rabble, a well-dressed, middle-aged couple sat at a corner table distastefully surveying their meal, the standard restaurant fare of calorie-laden burgers with chips, gravy, and bad coffee.

Irritated by the behaviour of the diners at the next table, the man beckoned to a passing staff member and said: "I would like to speak to the manager."

Pointing proudly at the name tag on his corporate jacket, the 20-year-old, pimple-faced staff member came to attention and said: "I am Willi Brandt, the assistant manager. How can I help you, Sir?"

Indicating the table next to them the man said, "Those lads are very noisy, they are spoiling our meal, please ask them to tone it down."

The lads he referred to were three of Willi's classmates from the Academy, Zachary Dillon, Eugene Hall, and Oska Wilde. "Certainly Sir, Willi replied."

Willi approached their table and said, "boys, you need to talk quietly. Tone down, you are upsetting the gentleman and lady at the next table."

The boys were in high spirits and were in no mood to tone down. They looked across at the couple at the next table and Eugene proclaimed loudly, "Why should we tone it down, this is our joint."

Willi knew what his friends were like in situations like this.

They thrived on belligerence, so he decided to try to bribe them into submission. He made his way to the kitchen and returned with a large plate of steaming chips and gravy, placing it in front of them, he said, "Chips on the house boys." The boys smiled their thanks but then Zac began to thump the table with his fists and shout, "Willi, Willi, Willi…" His two friends joined in. Willi sighed, he had done his best, and he quickly made himself scarce.

The couple had had enough of the unhealthy food and bad manners of their fellow diners. They got up and started to leave. The boys noticed this and changed their table-thumping chant to, "Leaving, leaving, leaving!"

Overcome by the boorishness of the boy's behaviour, the lady began to cry. Her husband quickly ushered her out of the restaurant, but not before he had taken a good look at Zac and his mates.

"I wonder who they were?" Eugene said.

"Dunno, but that guy must be pretty dumb bringing his wife to a joint like this," Zac replied.

"Probably just passing through," Oska said.

"Yeah, just passing through," Eugene agreed.

The following Monday at morning assembly the Headmaster introduced everybody to Mr Benson. He was the relief Master for Mr Buckmaster who was on sick leave. Mr Benson was a tall man who cut an imposing figure in his academic gown and mortarboard cap. He had a thin moustache and the disdainful look of a man used to being respected and having his way. "I am very grateful that Mr Benson has been able to join us at short notice," the Headmaster said.

At his last school, Mr Benson's students had given him the nickname bend over Benson for his propensity to apply the rod of correction to their backsides at the slightest provocation.

"Eugene, that's the dude from the restaurant!" Oska whispered.

"Fuck, I think that you are right," Eugene replied. They shifted their positions so that they were out of Mr Benson's view. Unfortunately, Zac was very tall and easily spotted among the crowd.

The Headmaster escorted Mr Benson into their classroom, introduced him and said, "Please give Mr Benson your full cooperation. It is not easy for a Master to take over a new class midterm."

The boys looked at Mr Benson decked out in his academic attire, taking the air of a supercilious Master, and tried not to smirk – he was a caricature of himself.

After the Headmaster had left, Mr Benson surveyed the twelve students in front of him. His eyes settled on Dillon. Pointing his finger at him, he said, "You! What is your name?"

"Freshman Zachary Dillon Sir."

"Step forward, Dillon."

Zac moved to the front of the classroom and stood before Mr Benson. "You are one of the louts who were so rude to my wife and I at the restaurant, isn't that right."

"Yes Sir," Zac replied.

"Where are the other two?" Mr Benson asked. Zac shrugged his shoulders and remained silent.

Mr Benson's face reddened with anger. "Don't try dumb insolence with me, Dillon, you are in enough trouble already," Zac stared straight ahead.

Eugene spoke up, "I was there, Sir."

"Name?" Mr Benson asked.

"Freshman Eugene Hall, Sir."

"Step forward Hall."

Word of the lad's act of buffoonery at the restaurant had got around the student fraternity and it was regarded unsympathetically. As Hall approached his fate, Freshman James, the class captain, whispered to him, "You guys are so busted. You'd better get butt naked as soon as you can."

Mr Benson looked around the room for the last culprit. "There was a third lad, identify yourself now or I will punish the whole class."

Oska stood up and said, "Freshman Oska Wilde, Sir."

Wanting to show solidarity with his friends, Willi also stood up and said, "Freshman Willi Brandt, assistant manager at the Bur…"

Before he could finish speaking, he was interrupted by Mr Benson who said, "I know, I know. Sit down Brandt, you did nothing wrong."

Willi sat down gratefully. He did not share his friend's propensity to behave badly and then suffer the inevitable consequences.

Mr Benson made them line up facing the class with their hands on their heads. "You ruined our meal, made my wife cry and disgraced yourselves and the Academy by your boorish behavior," he said. "What do you have to say for yourselves?"

They knew that Mr Benson was right, they hung their heads.

Speaking for all of them, Dillon said, "We have no excuse, Sir."

Mr Benson gave them their punishment. "You are to receive six strokes of the cane, naked of course, and you are to present yourselves to my wife and apologise to her for your loutish behaviour. This will be done after chapel on Sunday."

"Yes Sir," they all mumbled.

Mr Benson looked around the front of the classroom.

"Sir, the canes are in the cupboard to the right of the blackboard," Dillon said.

Mr Benson searched through the collection of punishment implements in the cupboard and selected a light rattan cane with a crooked handle. He gave it a practice swing; it scythed through the air with a loud, satisfying Swish. Then he looked at the three robust lads who were about to receive it and decided that it was too light. He settled on a three-foot-long medium rattan with a straight handle. He told the lads to prepare themselves for punishment – that usually meant to take everything off – and he removed his academic gown, mortarboard cap and his jacket.

Once they were totally naked and humbled before their peers, he told them to line up on the raised teacher's platform and to space themselves well apart.

"Bend over," he ordered.

They immediately and bent over.

The class watched these preparations with rising interest and excitement. A good class caning was always a stimulating diversion from lectures. They took in the magnificent spectacle of the three young men's well-presented bottoms, thrusting upwards waiting for punishment.

Mr Benson positioned himself next to Wilde. He tapped his bottom with his cane in preparation for the first stroke. Instinctively Wilde clenched his butt cheeks – such a nice sight. Mr Benson tapped his bottom again and said, "Relax your cheeks, Wilde."

Mr Benson then lifted the cane as far back as he could and swung it forward forcefully. The cane scythed through the air with an angry swish, and it cut across Wilde's waiting bottom with a loud crack.

"Ouch!" Wilde cried out. The first stroke always hurts more than expected.

Mr Benson allowed time for Wilde to appreciate the punitive effects of the stroke before applying the next. It landed across his bottom with another loud crack.

"Ouch, Ouch!" Wilde cried again as he moved his bottom up and down and clenched and unclenched his butt cheeks to try and alleviate the sting.

"Get back in position Wilde, bottom high," Mr Benson said. Wilde reluctantly assumed the correct position pushing his bottom up. "Good, hold that position," Mr Benson said, and he laid the next stroke across Wilde's throbbing bottom.

"Ouch, Ouch, Ouch!" An intense pain was building up across Wilde's bottom and instinctively his bare feet tapped out a dance on the floor. He was breathing heavily and starting to sweat, even though he was in the nude.

"Get back in position and stay there Wilde!" Mr Benson said savagely. "Your penis is flopping in a unacceptable way!"

"Yes Sir," Wilde sniffed.

Mr Benson gave Wilde three more strokes. He was not an accurate caner and, sometimes, he landed the cane across a previously caned spot. When this happened, it elicited a loud shriek from Wilde and caused his buttocks and legs to quiver uncontrollably. He repeatedly clenched his butt cheeks.

The caning over, Mr Benson said, "Stay in that position Wilde. No covering, hands behind your head."

"Yes Sir," Wilde said as he tried to control the tremor in his voice, his eyes were wet with tears.

Mr Benson then turned his attention to Hall who was anxiously waiting for his punishment to be over. Like Wilde, Hall was a slightly built young man with a similar tolerance to the pain inflicted by the cane. As Mr Benson laid the six swinging strokes across his bottom, he squirmed tapped his feet and his cries grew louder as the punishment progressed. By the end, he was sweating heavily, and his tears flowed freely. He was told to remain in position presenting his freshly pink, rose, and red caned bottom to his classmates.

Some of Hall's classmates stared salaciously at his tight bottom; their manhood's stirred.

Mr Benson then turned his attention to Dillon. He was starting to develop a particular dislike for him, he thought that he was far too cocky for his good. Dillon pushed his bottom out, and his underpants stretched snugly around his well-rounded orbs revealing the deep cleavage between them.

Dillon was a well-built young man with a tough hide. He was determined not to display signs of weakness. The first stroke scythed across his exposed bottom with a loud Crack. The pain was excruciating but he remained in the punishment position, and he took it without outcry. As the caning progressed and the pain built up Dillon started to sweat, his breathing became laboured, and his nostrils flared. But he didn't cry out, except when Mr Benson's cane landed across a previously caned spot on his throbbing bottom. Then his lower body spasmed violently and he grunted.

"Stand up, all of you," Mr Benson said.

They stood up awkwardly and immediately grabbed their smarting bottoms and tried to rub the pain away. Dillon's face was flushed. Tears ran down Hall and Wilde's faces. They walked the walk of shame as they returned to their seats, pretending not to notice the smirks on their classmate's faces as they looked at them sitting without clothes.

It was not a good week for Mr Benson. He struggled to master his young-adult pupils who, unlike the boys he was used to teaching, were sceptical and questioning about his teachings. He started to doubt himself. He fell back on his traditional methods of maintaining discipline and by the end of the week, he had caned every lad in the class with hours and hours of forced nudity.

Mr Benson was surprised to find that the Academy had a choir and that Dillon, Hall and Wilde were choristers. The choir sang hymns at the service on Sunday morning. They sang beautifully, their voices resonated around the chapel evoking genuine emotions among the congregation.

They sing like angels and behave like devils, a Master was heard to say.

After the service, Mr Benson and his wife, Angela, waited for Dillon and his friends outside the chapel. When they appeared, Mr Benson beckoned them over. They approached reluctantly. "Introduce yourselves to my wife and apologise to her," he told them.

No one wanted to go first so Dillon pushed Hall to the front.

"Good morning Ma'am. My name is Freshman Eugine Hall, and I am deeply sorry for my behaviour in the restaurant, and I apologise," he said, blushing.

Mrs Benson replied, "Thank you for your apology, Eugene, and I accept it," she gently touched Eugene's arm. "Is it true that my husband has spanked you totally naked in front of your classmates?"

"Y-yes, ma'am."

"Oh, that must have been a sight."

Dillon and Wilde made similar apologies.

Offering the boys an olive branch, Mrs Benson said, "We were two strange fish in your pond boys."

"More like a swamp," Mr Benson said scornfully. Mrs Benson glared at her husband; it had been his idea to go to that restaurant.

"You boys sang beautifully this morning," Mrs Benson said.

"Thank you, Ma'am."

Although the boys had done what he asked and apologised, Mr Benson was unhappy with the outcome of their meeting. He had expected his wife, who was a teacher at a senior boy's high school, to force-feed them a dose of humble pie, but instead, they had charmed their way into her heart and won her approval. "Let's get out of this place," he said to his wife.

Dillon noticed that Mr Benson never had a good word to say about the Academy or any of them and he wondered what he really thought of them.

On Monday Mr Benson made his way to the classroom with a heavy heart, he had not been sleeping well and he had allowed his students to occupy his head rent-free. He looked around the class, and he noticed that Dillon was sitting back nonchalantly in his chair with his hands behind his head, the front of his blazer was undone, and he was not wearing his tie.

"Dillon, why aren't you wearing your tie?"

Dillon shrugged his shoulders, "I forgot to put it on."

Mr Benson's face turned red with anger. "Approach the front of the class, Dillon. What sort of Academy man comes to class incorrectly attired?"

Dillon shrugged. He was as tall as Mr Benson and he could look him straight in the eye.

"How dare you behave in such an insolent manner? You are going to suffer for this!" Mr Benson said. "It is obvious that six of the best was not enough for you, so I will make it a dozen, across your bare bottom." He added. He picked up his cane.

Dillon shook his head. "No Sir, I will not accept chastisement from you." He eyeballed his Master holding his gaze.

Mr Benson's lower lip quivered and his right eye twitched. He lowered his eyes.

Dillon had won the contest of wills. He turned away and started to make his way back to his seat.

Mr Benson was overcome with anger. Spittle erupted from his mouth as he shouted, "This place is not an academic institution! It is a reform school for losers." The moment that the words left his mouth, he regretted saying them. He had just told his students exactly what he thought of them.

A sullen silence descended over the students. Mr Benson had hit them where it hurt. Most of them had chequered pasts, and the Academy was their last chance.

Somebody began to clap slowly, soon they were all clapping and shouting, "Dillon, Dillon, Dillon!"

Mr Benson realised that he lost the respect of his students and that there was no turning back. He flung his cane onto the floor.

Suddenly the classroom door opened, and the Headmaster walked in, he said, "What on earth is going on in here?" The lads fell silent and quickly got to their feet.

Mr Benson packed his papers into his briefcase. He turned and faced the headmaster, he had the eyes of a broken man. "Sorry Headmaster but I have better things to do with my time." He walked out.

The Headmaster was icily calm as he faced the class. He said, "Class captain?" Freshman James raised his hand. He told him that he was in charge of the class and that they were to remain at their desks.

They sat at their desks taking in what had just happened.

James turned to Dillon and said, "You did that deliberately, Dillon. You knew that he would crack."

Dillon shrugged his shoulders. It is good when a plan comes together, he thought.

"Now what will happen to us, we no longer have a teacher," James added.

"We aren't going to learn anything from a man who thinks we are worthless," Dillon replied. "He can spank me naked but he will never break me."

It was an hour before the Headmaster returned. They all stood up when he entered the classroom. "Sit down boys, while you still can." He said icily.

He told them that Mr Benson had left the Academy and would not be returning. He said, "You should all think about the part that you have played in destroying the career of a resolute teacher who has devoted his working life to the education and training of young men."

The lads lowered their heads and gazed at their desks, they felt ashamed of themselves.

He went on to tell them that he would be their Form Master until Mr Buckmaster returned from sick leave. "I expect a lot more cooperation from you than you gave to Mr Benson," he said.

He looked around the classroom. "Stand up Hall."

Hall stood.

"Strip naked. Go to my office, and fetch the strap. In this order."

"Yes Sir."

CHAPTER 5

Prefect attitudes

It was Saturday afternoon, and the lads were doing their weekly laundry. Three of them, Zachary Dillon, Eugene Hall, and Oska Wilde were making the task a team effort. Arriving at the laundry they discovered that all four washing machines were in use and a long queue had formed.

"This is bullshit," Zac said, and he decided to try the prefect's laundry on the next level of the dormitory block. They found that all three washing machines in the laundry were not being used and immediately claimed them. They had walked past a large sign at the entrance to the laundry which read: "ATTENTION, this laundry is for the use of Academy prefects only and it is out of bounds to all other students."

They loaded the machines up, one for socks and jocks, one for whites, and one for coloured clothes, started them, and left. They retired to Hall's room to collaborate on a homework assignment.

Sometime later they were interrupted by the Head Prefect, David Davenport, who asked them why they were using the prefect's laundry in contravention of Academy rules.

Hall was in an argumentative mood. He said, "Is it too much to ask that we be allowed to use your vacant washing machines if ours are being used?"

Davenport had been a student at the Academy for two years. He was twenty-two years old, a well-built lad who was academically sound and a good all-rounder in the sporting arena. He had been chosen for the demanding role of head prefect because he had shown a good commitment to Academy values and displayed good representational skills. He had also demonstrated good common sense and the ability to be patient, fair, understanding, and approachable.

"Is it too much to ask that you three obey the Academy rules?" Davenport replied. Looking straight at Hall he added, "The rules apply to everyone, Hall, which includes you."

Hall winced; the barb had struck home.

Davenport knew that the Academy rules and disciplinary procedures had been written with eighteen-year-olds in mind and that they grated with twenty-something lads like Dillon, Hall, and Wilde. Until now, he had cut them some slack, but he had warned them last week about using the prefect's laundry and they had ignored his warning. This time they had gone too far, and consequences were needed.

"You three need a lesson in obedience, report to the prefect's common room in ten minutes wearing your rugby kit and white underpants," he said.

The boys looked at each other in disbelief. The prefect system at the Academy was anathema to them. Having fellow students who were the same age or younger, with the power to discipline them, offended their sense of manhood. To Hall, his dislike of the prefect system was also stoked by his anti-authoritarian attitude. He seethed with barely concealed anger whenever he had dealings with a prefect.

Rebellion fomented in the minds of Hall and Wilde, but Dillon knew that a circumspect approach was required. They had broken the Academy rules and therefore, deserved punishment. Also, any attempt to challenge the prefect's authority would attract severe consequences.

"We have to cop it sweet boys, let's get it over with and show them that we can take our thrashings like men."

"I think that it sucks," Hall complained.

Dillon, who held sway over both his friends, gave Hall his dominant look, and Hall fell into line.

They presented themselves at the prefect's common room. The room covered a large area, including a lounge with a TV, comfortable Chesterfield sofas, a billiard table, and refreshment facilities. It also contained a punishment area with a line of four evenly spaced desks used for bending over, a row of canes hanging from hooks on the wall, and an end table holding an elaborately bound punishment book. Each desk had a small side table to hold the punishment lad's clothing.

Davenport and two prefects met them; all three young men were stripped down to their waists displaying their muscular physiques. Below the waist, they were clad in Academy attire: bone moleskin trousers, brown R.M Williams boots, and a one-and-a-half-inch double-butt leather belt with brass hardware. Each held a long, medium-weight rattan cane in his hand striking an arrogant pose with the cane's tip resting on the floor. Their faces tilted upwards – a sign of intimidation.

The punishment lads wore blue rugby jerseys with the Academy logo on the front and their names on the back, tight-fitting, white rugby shorts, and black leather boots.

Davenport took the three lads in hand; he told them to stand in front of a desk and to strip down to their underpants. They reluctantly obeyed folding their clothing neatly on the side table. He positioned Prefect Hart opposite Hall and Prefect Harding opposite Wilde. He stood opposite Dillon. "It is six of the best for all of you," he said.

"Only on their underpants, Davenport?" Harding asked.

"Yes, on their underpants," Davenport replied. Harding looked disappointed.

Harding and Hart looked at their victims with a keen sense of anticipation, in their view they were arrogant upstarts who, if it hadn't been for Davenport providing them with top cover, would have received a prefect's thrashing long ago.

Wilde and Harding eyeballed each other, there was no love lost between them. Wilde was unashamedly gay, and this angered Harding who was an all-in redneck.

Presumptuously, Wilde held Harding's gaze and he reacted angrily. "Don't eyeball me, Wilde. I am going to thrash your arse," he spat.

Davenport reacted immediately, "Stow that language, Harding, and apologize to Wilde."

"I am not going to apologize to some f–"

Before he could finish, Wilde interrupted him and said to Davenport, "It's ok, Davenport, it is the truth, I know who I am." Looking at Harding he continued, "But I don't jerk off in the shower with my roomies and pretend that I am straight."

Harding exploded, "Fuck you, Wilde! That's going to cost you another six."

"No, it is not, and you are stood down Harding," Davenport said.

"What?"

"You heard me. Hang up your cane and go and stand in front of the spare desk, you need a lesson in Academy values. We respect all students irrespective of who they are," he said.

"Are you taking his side, Davenport?" Harding asked incredulously.

"In this instance, Harding, yes I am."

Davenport told Harding to strip down to his underpants. Harding removed his boots and trousers, revealing that he was not wearing any.

"Why aren't you wearing underpants? They are part of your uniform, Harding."

Harding looked at his mate Hart and their faces flushed red.

"Well Harding?" Davenport asked.

Looking sheepish, Harding said, "Um, well, we decided to go commando today, Davenport."

"Why?" Davenport asked.

"Um, it's like a silent act of defiance against Academy rules," he said.

Dillon, Hall, and Wilde all smirked.

Davenport sighed; this prefect was proving troublesome. "You are to receive six licks of your belt for your lack of Academy values and an extra lick for going commando. Now hand me your belt and bend over."

Harding handed Davenport his double-butt leather belt and bent right over the desk. He was buck-naked.

"Spread your legs wide and push your butt out, Davenport said."

Harding complied and his muscular butt mooned invitingly. All eyes were on his olive skin with no tan line, his smooth well-rounded orbs, and his lush growth of pubic hair defining his crack and covering his manhood. The anxiety he felt caused his heart to race and he sweated freely.

Davenport grasped the belt by the buckle end and began to lay it across Harding's bottom. Each lick landed with a sharp *Crack!* and caused Harding to yelp loudly. He made Harding count off each lick, as his penis danced forward and back, getting a bit hard.

"Hold your penis with your hand. It's moving too much, this is not an adult show."

"Yes, sir. Sorry sir." And so Harding held his penis with his right hand, which only made it grow harder.

When he had given him six, Davenport paused. "Now an extra one for not wearing your underpants, Harding."

"Oh, yes, Davenport," he sniffed.

Davenport gave him one more lick, the hardest of the series, which made Harding jump and take his hand away from his crotch. Davenport pretended not to see that his penis was now straight as a dancing pole. "Now let that be a lesson, Harding," he said.

Harding stood up and grabbed his smarting butt cheeks, not caring to show his raging boner. His face was as red as his bruised bottom. Davenport made him stand naked facing the wall with his hands on his head.

Dillon smirked. "A disciplinary caning which was supposed to be conducted with appropriate decorum was descending into high farce. It is about time you pulled your boy into line, Davenport," he said.

Davenport didn't ignore him and said, "I won't tolerate this from you. Bend over the desk Dillon. And no more joking."

Dillon bent right over the desk and, stretching his arms forward, grasped the railing at the back. Davenport's eyes widened as he noticed that Dillon was wearing his white, gym-issue jockstrap and not his underpants as he had instructed.

"Why aren't you wearing your white underpants, Dillon?"

"All my undies are in your washing machine, Davenport,"

he replied. He knew that while underpants would protect his modesty they would do little to protect his bottom from the onslaught of Davenport's cane.

"That will cost you an extra stroke Dillon," Davenport said.

"Yes, Davenport."

Davenport eyed Dillon's bottom. The straps stretched tightly over his well-rounded, muscular orbs, it was raised high in a perfect position to receive the cane. He nodded his head approvingly. "Hold that position, Dillon."

Davenport selected a spot about a third of the way from the top of Dillon's ample buttocks and tapped it twice with his cane. He then let fly with the first stroke. The cane scythed through the air with a loud Swish and struck his bare bottom with a loud *Crack!* Dillon gasped from the shock of the stroke. "It hurt!"

Davenport allowed enough time to elapse for the punitive effects of the stroke to be absorbed before he laid on the next stroke. It landed across Dillon's bottom with another loud *Crack!*

"Ouch, ouch!" he exclaimed.

Dillon received five more full-strength strokes of the cane. He gasped, writhed on the desktop, and stretched his legs out to try and alleviate the smarting sting, but he always pushed his butt back into the punishment position in a timely fashion to receive the next stroke. Each stroke left a thin white line across his bottom which turned pink before developing into an angry red welt. He started to sweat, and his breathing became laboured.

"Stand up Dillon," Davenport said. Dillon stood awkwardly and he immediately grabbed his smarting arse cheeks and rubbed them fiercely trying to rub away the pain.

Davenport extended his hand. No hard feelings, Dillon.

Dillon grasped his extended hand and said, "No hard feelings, thanks for the lesson Davenport."

Then, Davenport told him to face the wall and place his hands on his head.

Davenport told Prefect Hart to cane Hall. "Give him six of the best, Hart, he said."

"Bend over the desk, Hall", Hart said.

Hall bent over as instructed and, without being told, he wriggled his body across the desk, spread his legs, and raised his bottom high into the correct punishment position. He felt his underpants stretch tightly around his butt cheeks and genitals.

Hart grunted his satisfaction at the sight of Hall's well-presented bottom. He swung his cane and it landed with a crack across Hall's sit spot, the crease between his bottom and his upper legs.

"Ouch!" Hall cried. Hart delivered the next stroke; it cracked across the back of Hall's calves. Hall winced and yelped with shock. It was clear that Hart did not know how to give the cane. Hall's anxiety mounted and he began to sweat profusely.

Davenport interrupted Hart and gave him a short lesson in the art of using the cane. He ran his finger across Hall's bottom and said, "You must cane him on his underpants. Pick the spot that you want to strike, and then tap that spot with your cane – do it," he said.

Hart complied.

"Now keep your eye on that spot and swing the cane."

Hart landed a good stroke near the spot that he had selected.

"Ouch, ouch!" Hall cried.

"Good. That's how you cane a naughty student's bottom, Hart," Davenport said.

"Thanks, Davenport," Hart replied.

Dillon watched Hall's caning with mounting frustration. He said, "Davenport, Hall is not a training aid. If your prefect can't use the cane, you should find someone who can."

Davenport flushed with anger. He saw Dillon's comments as an attempt to usurp his authority. "The prefects have to learn somehow, and if you interfere again Dillon I will report you to the duty Master," he snapped.

Dillon fell silent.

Gaining confidence, Hart gave Hall three more well-delivered strokes. "Stand up Hall," he said.

Hall stood up awkwardly. He quickly wiped the tears from his face with the back of his hand, and he then rubbed his smarting bottom.

Extending his hand, Hart said, "No hard feelings, Hall." It was considered good form to shake hands after a caning. Hall accepted his hand reluctantly but did not reply.

Davenport then picked up his cane and told Wilde to assume the position over the desk. Anxious to get it done, Wilde quickly bent right over the desk and wriggled his arse into position. His bottom mooned, inviting punishment. Davenport then gave him six blistering strokes across his tight underpants. Wilde received his strokes as stoically as possible with little outcry. The seat of Wilde's underpants was well worn, and the results of his caning could be discerned under the thin cotton cloth.

The musky scent of sweating young men permeated the room.

"Stand up, Wilde," Davenport said. Wilde rubbed his bottom vigorously. Davenport extended his hand. "No hard feelings, Wilde."

Wilde accepted the handshake. "No hard feelings, Davenport, and thanks for speaking up for me," he said.

Davenport nodded. "It is my job."

Davenport entered the details of the punishments in the prefect's punishment book, all three punishment lads then had to acknowledge the receipt of their punishment by signing the book.

Dillon was having second thoughts about his unhelpful interventions during the punishment. He said, "I am sorry for my attitude, Davenport. I was out of line."

Davenport was disappointed with Dillon's attitude. He said, "You should think ahead, Dillon. Next year, when I leave the Academy, you may be appointed head prefect, and then it will be you who has to deal with a bunch of truculent lads and demanding Masters."

Dillon shook his head. "No chance of that, my rap sheet is too long."

"You don't get it, Dillon. They don't care about your conduct record, you will still get thrashed when you incur your Master's displeasure. They will want you for your leadership skills and experience."

Dillon lapsed into a thoughtful silence.

"Now, you three," Davenport said, addressing the three culprits. "Since you were so eager to use our washing machines, it's only fair that you are allowed to do it after taking the punishment so bravely. Even because it seems you have one more item of clothing to wash, each." The three could clearly see where this was going. "Strip of your underwear now, walk to our washing machines, and put them together with the rest. In this order. You will wait naked for the end of the washing, standing in the corridor with your hands behind your head, and will remain like that whoever comes by."

The three obeyed, stripping in front of the prefects. They did as instructed, then, after about two hours, they returned to their dorm. Hall, and Wilde looked dejected, crushed by the experience. The main sting of the punishment was caused by humiliation and not the bruises on their bottoms.

Dillon knew that they needed cheering up. He stood between them and hugged them both, "Cheer up, boys, at least Davenport didn't give us detention, so we can hit the town tonight. A good night out will soothe our bruised egos, and when we get back we can salve each other's bruised bottoms, and deal with any other issues that may arise."

The boys grinned knowingly.

CHAPTER 6

Public canings at morning assemblies were rare events at the Standfast Academy. But the Headmaster, Dr Barton had decided that a group of students' behaviour was so heinous that, in the interests of good academy discipline, they merited a public thrashing. Six students were up for punishment, they were:

Head Prefect, David Davenport, 24 years old.
Prefect, Nathan College, 24 years old.
Prefect, Glenn Maris, 23 years old.
Prefect, Benjamin Racal, 22 years old.
Senior, Gregory Otter, 22 years old.
Freshman, Zachary Dillon, 25 years old.

News about the grand opening of Suzie's Bar and Massage Parlour was a first for the university town of Banks. It had caused quite a stir among the conservative, God-fearing locals. Flyers advertising the opening night were sent to all pubs, businesses, and places of entertainment. They were also sent to the seats of higher learning in Banks including the Standfast Academy. The flyers warmly welcomed guests and offered a happy hour and a chance to meet the bar girls in an informal setting.

The flyers began appearing on noticeboards in public places and the dorms throughout the Academy, creating great interest among the students. Dr Barton was enraged at the presence of the flyers on campus and staff and prefects were sent on search-and-destroy missions to remove them.

Suzie's bar was declared off-limits to students and the prohibition was advised in writing in Academy routine orders and verbally at morning assemblies.

When he issued this proclamation, the headmaster considered the reputational damage that the presence of academy students at Suzie's bar would do to the Academy. He was also conscious of the duty of care that the Academy has for the safety of its students given the possibility of physical and moral harm associated with attendance at places like Suzie's bar and massage parlour.

Acts of defiance among young men subject to strict discipline are a normal, healthy response to arbitrary prohibitions. The headmaster's decision to put Suzie's bar off-limits invited pushback, especially from the more worldly and naturally defiant lads.

The six young Standfast men were welcomed by Suzie and her girls, and they stayed at Suzie's place until 01:00 hours on Saturday morning. When they arrived back at the Academy, the Head Porter, Mr Seeking, informed them that they were to report to the duty master at 08:00 hours the next morning in full Academy uniform.

The lads had felt confident that their attendance at Suzie's bar had gone undetected by the Academy authorities. They were taken aback by the requirement to report to the Duty Master.

"What is all this about, Sir?" Davenport asked.

Mr Seeking said, "I am passing on instructions that I received from the Duty Master, Mr Buckmaster. That is all I can say."

The next morning the lads reported to Mr Buckmaster. He was not in good humour. "Did you lot attend the opening night at Suzie's bar last night?" he asked.

The lads looked at each other. "How do you know that, Sir? Davenport asked."

"The headmaster told me. You are all grounded for the remainder of the weekend, and you are to present yourselves to him at morning assembly on Monday for a very public thrashing," Mr Buckmaster said.

The lads were in shock. "How did he find out, Sir?" Davenport asked.

"Were you asked to provide ID?" Mr Buckmaster asked.

"No Sir, but we did have to complete and sign a declaration that we were legally adults," Dillon said.

"You provided false names and addresses of course," Mr Buckmaster said.

There was an embarrassed silence. Mr Buckmaster was angered by their naivety. His face reddened. "The headmaster is a friend of the company's manager who provided customer vetting and security services for Suzie's bar. That's how he found out," he said.

Mr Buckmaster was ambivalent about their behaviour. On the one hand, they had disobeyed the headmaster's directive but on the other hand, visiting a massage parlour was something that lads did. But he could not abide stupidity, especially from lads who were supposed to be smart.

"You deserve punishment for being so bloody stupid!" he roared. "Dillon, you remain behind, the rest of you get out of my sight!"

Mr Buckmaster was Dillon's form master and he decided that the time had come for them to have a Master/student conversation. Dillon had been at the Academy for a year, and his performance had been lacklustre. He did just enough academic work to achieve a passing grade in his assessments and he had shown a propensity to push the disciplinary boundaries and enthusiastically indulge in acts of defiance against Academy authority. His rap sheet was long. The one area where he excelled was in the sporting arena where he showed great promise.

Mr Buckmaster was a heavyset man who in his younger days had boxed and played rugby, his crooked nose was a testament to injuries he had received on the rugby pitch. He was physically intimidating even to robust lads like Dillon. He had a well-deserved reputation for being a strict disciplinarian and all twelve of the unruly lads in his form benefited from his tough love when he felt that they needed it. The lads thrived under his tough no-nonsense regime and a mutual respect had developed between the tough disciplinarian and his troublesome students.

"What possessed you to flout the headmaster's edict and attend Suzie's bar, Dillon?" he asked.

Dillon shook his head mournfully. "I don't know, Sir, it seemed like a good idea at the time."

"Bah! That is a pathetic answer Dillon, a young man your age with your service in the army should be demonstrating a more mature attitude. What sort of example are you setting for the younger lads?" he asked.

Dillon hung his head. Mr Buckmaster's criticism had struck home. "I am sorry, Sir. I don't understand why I do this stuff."

"The trouble with you Dillon is that you are too cocky and you think that Academy authority is beneath you." Mr Buckmaster admonished. "What you need is a forced feeding of humble pie to deflate that ego of yours," he continued.

"Oh Sir, your words are so harsh," Dillon complained.

Looking him in the eye, Mr Buckmaster said, "You need more than harsh words, Dillon, what you need is a man who knows how to talk to you and how to deal with you in a way that you understand."

"Yes, Sir," Dillon gulped.

"I have been too lenient with you, Dillon. So from now on, whenever you incur my displeasure, you will be receiving the benefit of my punishment strap across your bare bottom," he said.

Dillon looked his form Master in the eye and then submissively dropped his gaze. "You are right, I need to be thrashed regularly, Sir," he replied. The thought of regular thrashings from his tough form master made Dillon's manhood stir.

"As for your act of defiance on Friday night, you will receive your thrashing from the HM on Monday, Dillon. But for now, report to Mr Seeking. He has a grease trap that needs bailing out."

"A grease trap Sir?"

Mr Buckmaster gazed at him sternly. "Do you have a problem with that, Dillon?"

Dillon quickly replied, "No, Sir. Thank you, Sir."

Morning assemblies at the Academy were conducted in the open, the students assembled in classes in front of a raised dais with a set of stairs on each side.

When the punishment lads arrived, the student body was assembled, and the masters sat in a group on the left-hand side of the dais. A sturdy wooden table was in place at the centre of the dais and two, three-foot-long medium-weight rattan canes waited in a bucket beside the table.

The punishment lads, under the supervision of Mr Buckmaster, waited at the foot of the stairs. The headmaster opened the morning assembly with an announcement that the students awaiting punishment had defiantly disobeyed his instruction and had attended the opening night of Suzie's bar the previous Friday night.

"Each student will strip completely nude before us, then present himself at this table and will receive twelve strokes of the cane. He is also restricted to the Academy for the next two weekends," the headmaster said. "This is the maximum punishment that I am allowed to award in these circumstances," he added.

Turning to face the punishment lads he said, "Step forward, Davenport."

Davenport removed his blazer and handed it to the lad standing next to him, he then loosened his tie, took off his shoes and socks, and everything else. It was the first time he was nude before such a huge audience, and that made him shiver and sweat. Hoping he wouldn't get an erection, he mounted the steps to the dais, trying to think that he still had clothes on, with little success. All eyes were on his naked skin, and his genitals. He positioned himself facing the table with his back to the assembled students.

"Bend over, Davenport," the headmaster said.

Davenport's hands shook nervously as he bent right over the table, grasped the railing at the back, and wriggled his bottom into position with his head low and his bottom raised high. He felt his skin tighten around his muscular orbs, and knew that his anus was in sight.

The assembled students shifted their positions so that they could get an unobstructed view of Davenport's muscular, tight bottom and his impending thrashing. Many of them had erections.

Dr Barton was a fit, fifty-year-old man who had a lot of experience wielding the cane across young men's errant bottoms.

He had more than enough stamina to deal out an effective headmaster's thrashing to the six young miscreants. He removed his jacket, loosened his tie, and rolled up the shirtsleeve on his right arm. He then selected a cane and gave it two practice swings. It *thwipped* angrily through the air, and the students noticed that Davenport's buttock cheeks involuntarily spasmed.

The headmaster then selected a place on Davenport's bottom just below the top of his orbs and tapped it twice with his cane. He stepped back and delivered a full-strength stroke across that area.

A loud Thwip, was heard as the cane scythed through the air, quickly followed by a loud scream, as it impacted Davenport's bottom.

"Count," the headmaster said.

"One, Sir!" Davenport replied.

The headmaster allowed time for the impact of the stroke to be fully absorbed before delivering the next stroke.

Thwip.

"Two, sir!" The increasing pain caused Davenport to writhe on the table and lift his legs.

"Get your bottom back into position, Davenport," the headmaster said. "Or I'll keep you naked for the whole week."

Davenport knew that the students and the masters were watching him and that there was an expectation that he would take his punishment in a manly fashion with minimal corrections from the headmaster. He pushed his bottom back into position, and resolved to keep it there.

Thwip.

"Three, Sir." His voice quavered.

The headmaster continued to mete out the punishment, and as the pain continued to build up on Davenport's bottom, his body spasmed and he stretched his legs to resolve it.

Davenport's breathing became laboured and he began to sweat profusely.

Allowing time for the effects of each stroke to be absorbed, and to prolong the state of public nudity which was a great enforcement of his authority, it took the headmaster three minutes to cane Davenport. Finally, his ordeal was over. Davenport remained across the table. He was gasping for breath and tears of pain and shame filled his eyes.

"Stand up, Davenport," the headmaster said.

Davenport stood up awkwardly, he grasped his bottom with both hands and rubbed it, not caring about his exposed genitals.

The headmaster held out his hand and said, "No hard feelings Davenport. You took that well."

Davenport took the Headmaster's hand, and with a faltering voice said, "No hard feelings, Sir. Thanks for the lesson. Can I wear my clothes now?"

"No, I'm afraid not. You will stand by the side, still naked and with hands behind your head, until all your fellow students have been punished."

Under Mr Buckmaster's supervision, the mass punishment proceeded smoothly. The lads were organised in order of precedence with Davenport, the head prefect at the front of the line and Dillon at the back. One by one they stepped up totally naked to receive their punishment. The punished lads formed a separate line with their backs to the assembled students, and their hands on their heads.

Mr Buckmaster watched Dillon take his punishment. As the caning progressed his torment was betrayed by his quivering bare bottom and by the sound of his quavering voice as he counted off each stroke. Mr Buckmaster grimaced, 'A good lesson in humility will do Dillon the world of good,' he thought.

The assembled students watched the spectacle with mixed feelings, on the one hand, the salacious scenes of senior students receiving the cane across their bottoms pandered to the erotic side of their natures. At least two of them came in their pants, hoping it wouldn't show through. On the other hand, the punishment also served as a warning of what would happen to them should they misbehave. But some of them, in their erotic fantasies, just hoped to end up naked on the stage, to be displayed and punished just like that.

But mostly, a dark mood descended upon the student body.

That evening after lights out the six punishment lads secretly gathered in the prefect's shower room. As agreed, they arrived naked. They all needed to relieve their sexual tensions brought on by the thrashing that they had received from the headmaster that morning. Dillon was designated the activity supervisor. He lined them up with their hands on their heads. "Bend over and touch your toes lads," he said with a broad grin.

They all bent over immediately. He moved down the line of well-presented bottoms inspecting each lad's cane welts and black and blue bruises. He gently massaged each butt. When he had finished, they all sported firm erections.

He then formed them into a circle with one arm around the next lad's shoulder and the other hand holding their throbbing manhoods. "Ok, lads. Start stroking. The last one to spurt gets one hundred push-ups," he said. "Free cumming as always." They bent to their task with gusto, and soon they were shooting on each other's bare legs, with sperm dripping along their young skin and muscular bodies. Davenport was the last to cum, maybe intentionally. He had to do one hundred push-ups, but as they usually do, he had the other boys sit on the floor with their crotches right before his face, and he sucked their cocks clean as he pushed his body up and down. Two of them shot their cream again into Davenport's mouth. Dillon finally came on the lad's arse, shooting his white fluids all along his crack, before giving Davenport the privilege to clean his penis with his own mouth. Which of course had Davenport shooting again in a powerful orgasm.

At the next morning assembly, the students were surprised to see the same six lads lined up on the dais facing them. They stood tall with their feet apart and their hands behind their backs. Their confident demeanour masked their feelings of pain and humiliation caused by the thrashings that they had received the day before. The headmaster announced that Davenport, the head prefect, was going to make a public apology for the group's act of defiance. He beckoned him to step forward and handed him a prepared apology. Davenport folded it and placed it on the shelf under the rostrum. He intended to deliver the apology in his own words. This act of defiance was noticed by everybody at the assembly.

The headmaster's face flushed with anger when he realized that Davenport was not going to deliver the apology that he had prepared for him.

Although he had carefully prepared his words, Davenport felt extremely nervous. He stood stiffly on the rostrum and tightly gripped the base of the microphone. He stuttered as he began to speak but his voice steadied as he gained confidence.

"Good morning Headmaster, masters and fellow students. On behalf of myself and my fellow miscreants, I apologise for our defiant behaviour last Friday night. We did this in wilful defiance of the headmaster's express edict that Suzie's bar was off-limits to all Academy students. We knew it was wrong and if we were caught there would be severe consequences, so why did we do it? It is hard to provide a cogent reason for our behaviour. But young men of our age are predisposed to acts of bold disobedience. In other words, we stand up when the authorities order us to sit down. This is not offered as an excuse for our behaviour, there is no excuse. But it explains why we did it."

The headmaster's anger subsided, and he began to listen thoughtfully. Mr Buckmaster who was twiddling his big thumbs as he listened, nodded his head in agreement.

Davenport continued, looking at the headmaster he said, "Sir, it is my job as head prefect to function as a conduit between you, the headmaster and the students and to support you in enforcing discipline. In this instance, I have failed you and for that, I am deeply sorry."

Looking around at the students he said, "This is probably the last time that you will see me in my role as head prefect, given my behavior. I think that I will be demoted. I deserve to be. It is not a problem for the Academy because suitable candidates for the position abound. I know this because not a day goes by without me receiving free and frank advice about how I should do my job from any number of aspirants."

A titter of laughter ran through the ranks of assembled students.

"Finally, lads, if any of you are thinking of emulating our act of buffoonery – don't! Suzie's bar is overrated, and it is certainly not worth the punishment. Thank you."

There was a long silence while they absorbed what Davenport had said. Then there was laughter and applause.

Everybody liked Davenport after that.

Davenport stayed frozen in position in front of the microphone his hand gripping its base in a vice-like grip.

The headmaster tapped him on the shoulder and said. "You can stand down now, Davenport."

Davenport handed the headmaster his unread speech and respectfully stood aside.

The headmaster waved for silence, he said, "To dispel any doubts, Davenport will continue in the role of head prefect and he will report to my office immediately after this assembly."

More laughter erupted.

The lads dispersed into small groups keenly discussing the events of the last two days. Compared to the morning before their mood was much happier.

CHAPTER 7

A night on the town

It was a typically busy Friday evening at the Academy security gate as happy students jostled each other while leaving the campus for the evening. Freshmen Zac Dillon, Eugene Hall, and Oska Wilde were looking forward to a night out in Banks and a break from the strict Academy discipline. They joked around with Mr Reg Seeking, the head porter, as he signed them out. Reg knew the three lads well and, while he knew they needed a chance to let off some steam, he worried about their propensity to get themselves into trouble. He reminded them they were due back on campus no later than 23:00 hours that night and advised them to stay out of trouble.

"Yes Sir," they chorused. But Reg felt they were not listening, and he noticed that Dillon had his *looking for trouble* look in his eyes.

The cash-strapped lads knew how to eke out their money and they patronized the cheap venues; the bowling alley, the Banks cinema and ended the evening with a cheap cheeseburger and coffee deal at the Burger Treat restaurant.

As they sat in the restaurant, Dillon spotted three big, tough-looking lads seated at a nearby table. He recognized them as acquaintances from the rival St Andrew's rugby team.

"Boys!" he called out happily and they invited him to join them.

They had an animated conversation and Dillon quickly agreed to join them for a late night out at Suzie's Bar and Massage Parlour, even though he knew that Suzie's bar was off-limits to Academy students. During their conversation, Dillon pointed to Hall and Wilde and his three new friends turned and smirked at them. Then they left the restaurant. On his way out, Dillon said to Hall and Wilde, "I am joining these lads for the rest of the night, you two get your arses back to the Academy."

"Why can't we come with you?" Hall said.

"No, you can't come this is men's business. Besides you haven't been invited," Dillon said as he chased after his three new companions.

The boys were shocked by Dillon's behaviour. "I bet that they are going to Suzie's bar," Wilde said.

"I am disgusted, fucking disgusted," Hall said angrily. "I hope this earns him another public, naked, spanking."

Oska looked at his watch and said, "We had better hurry Eugene, or we will miss the last bus."

"Fuck the bus, I am not getting my arse back to the Academy just because Dillon tells me to," he said bitterly.

"But we will get into trouble, Eugene," Oska said.

"I don't care. I like being spanked naked anyway, and so do all of you. Let's be honest. Let's go to the pub and spend the rest of our money," Eugene said defiantly.

…

It was 7 am on Saturday. Eugene Hall and Oska Wilde stood before Magistrate Marcof Cain who was presiding over the early morning session of the Banks local court. Magistrate Cain was reading the lad's charge sheets that Constable Bull had prepared.

Finally, he looked at Hall, "Vagrancy, Mr Eugene," he said.

Hall looked at Constable Bull who was standing behind them. He shrugged his shoulders.

"My name is Hall, Eugene Hall, Sir."

"Ah yes, of course, Mr Hall. Sometimes the police officers put the names in the wrong boxes on the charge sheet," he said by way of explanation.

The constable rolled his eyes.

"It says here that at about 2 am this morning, you were found wandering in Kitchener Park. You were mildly intoxicated, you could not provide a valid reason for being in the park and you had no money on your person, is this correct?" The magistrate asked.

"Yes Sir," Hall replied.

"There is no crime in being *mildly intoxicated* but do you two have a home?" Magistrate Cain asked. The lads could smell the sour odour of stale wine wafting across the bench.

"Yes Sir, we are both students at the Standfast Academy," Hall replied.

The magistrate's demeanour changed. "Ah, Standfast Academy. I know your Headmaster, Dr Barton," he said. "The next time you are up before him please tell him that Magistrate Cain sends his regards."

"Yes Sir we will, but we try our best not to be up before our headmaster Sir," Wilde replied.

"A very sensible aim," the magistrate replied. "Does he still spank totally naked?"

"Yes, he does, Sir."

"I can understand why he does that." Turning to Constable Bull he asked, "Did they give you any trouble, constable?"

"No Sir. They were well-behaved, we only brought them in because we were concerned for their welfare," the constable replied.

"Quite right too, Kitchener Park is no place for young men like you to loiter in, especially after dark," the magistrate said.

The lads hung their heads. "Yes, Sir," they replied.

"When I was your age, lads like you who got themselves into trouble with the police would be sent down to the cell block underneath this courthouse and given twelve strokes of the birch rod across their bare bottoms," the magistrate said. "But that usually doesn't happen today, at least here," he added with a smile.

The lads shifted uncomfortably as they conjured up images of what it would have been like to have their bare bottoms thrashed with a birch rod.

The magistrate looked at Hall and Wilde sternly. "Well-behaved young men do not come to the attention of the police," he said. He then decided, "I am going to send you two lads back to your Academy, with your charge sheets. There, you are to report to your headmaster or his representative and he will decide how to deal with you. Even though I can already see what he will decide to do. Case dismissed," the magistrate declared.

"Thank you, Sir," the boys replied.

Mr Seeking was relieved to see Hall and Wilde even if they were under escort by Constable Bull of the Banks Police Department. The constable handed the boy's charge sheets to Mr Seeking and explained what needed to happen.

"I will ensure that the magistrate's instructions are carried out Constable, and thanks for bringing the lads back," he said.

The constable nodded at Hall and Wilde and said, "Good luck boys."

"Thank you, Constable," they smiled weakly.

Mr Seeking asked them, "Where is Dillon?"

"We don't know, Sir, he went off with some mates from the St Andrew's rugby club," Hall said.

Mr Seeking told the lads to go to their dorm, get cleaned up and report to the duty master in uniform. "You lads are in serious trouble," he said. "But you already know."

Feeling sorry for themselves, they replied, "Yes Sir."

He then sent for the duty prefect. He was surprised when Davenport, the head prefect reported to him.

"Why are you pulling duty prefect, Davenport?" he asked.

"It is punishment for defying the headmaster and using my own words to make the public apology at morning assembly after we visited Suzie's bar a few weeks ago. I copped duty prefect last weekend and this weekend, Sir," he replied. "I am learning the hard way, Sir," he added with a rueful smile.

Mr Seeking's eyes twinkled. He had noticed that Davenport was becoming more assertive and was challenging Academy authority. He was growing up.

"Learning the hard way is the best way to learn, Davenport," Mr Seeking said with a smile. He continued, "I called you because I want you to find Dillon and have him report to me as soon as possible."

"Yes Sir," Davenport replied. "With or without clothes?"

"You decide."

...

Hall and Wilde stood before Mr Buckmaster, the duty master, as he read the report that Mr Seeking had submitted and the police charge sheets.

He noted in the timeline that Mr Seeking submitted that Dillon, Hall and Wilde had left the Academy together at 18:00 hrs on Friday evening, and that at 09:00 hrs this morning Wilde and Hall were returned to the Academy by constable Bull from the Banks Police Department. Mr Buckmaster noted that there was no record of Dillon returning to the Academy.

"Where is Dillon, why isn't he with you?" he asked. The boys shook their heads in silence.

"You boys are in enough trouble. Don't make it worse by committing dumb insolence," he said.

"We separated during the evening, and he went his way, Sir," Hall replied.

Mr Buckmaster felt that Dillon's absence was significant to the matter at hand, but he decided to let that stand for now. His face reddened in anger as he read the police report.

"Arrested for vagrancy, appearing before the magistrate at the Banks local court, what a disgrace!" he thundered. He glared at Hall and Wilde. He was shocked and angered by their behaviour. "Your actions have dishonoured the academy and yourselves," he said.

The boys hung their heads in shame.

He awarded Hall and Wilde their punishment. "You are both to receive twelve strokes of the strap, six across your underpants and six on your bare bottoms. In addition, you are grounded for the rest of the weekend."

"Thank you, Sir," the lads chorused.

"Strip down to your underpants and boots," Mr Buckmaster said.

They obeyed, neatly folding their clothes and placing them on a desk.

Mr Buckmaster then indicated two desks alongside each other and told the lads to assume a position standing in front of them with their hands on their heads. He then rummaged in his cupboard and produced his black, double leather, eighteen-inch punishment strap, the strap had a 2-layer, stitched handle.

He showed it to the boys. "This will take some skin off your backsides," he told them.

The boy's eyes widened, and they shifted their positions uncomfortably.

"Bend right over the desk," he ordered.

The boys knew the procedure. Each lad bent over his desk and grabbed the legs at the back for support, pushed his head down and raised his backside into the correct punishment position.

Mr Buckmaster ran his master's hand over each lad's tight underpants to smooth out wrinkles, before picking up his strap and tapping their bottoms with it. "Move your legs further apart," he said. The boy's bottoms mooned invitingly as they waited nervously for what was coming to them.

Starting with Hall, Mr Buckmaster laid three hard strokes of the strap across the seat of his tight, white underpants. The events leading up to his current predicament had left Hall feeling distraught. He didn't hold back but hollered loudly with the rise and fall of the strap across his quivering bottom.

Mr Buckmaster then turned his attention to Wilde and gave him the same treatment. Wilde gasped and groaned as he absorbed the bruising sting of the strap.

Mr Buckmaster then turned his attention back to Hall. "Get your bottom up, tight underpants," he ordered. Reluctantly Hall pushed his smarting bottom back into position and he received three more blistering strokes. He cried out loudly and his feet tapped out a dance on the floor.

Mr Buckmaster then gave Wilde three more hard licks he gasped and cried out but tried to receive his punishment in a manly fashion.

Speaking to both lads, Mr Buckmaster said, "Stand up and remove your underpants. I want to see you naked, afraid and crying, or I won't stop."

The lads obeyed leaving their underpants on the floor. Both lads wiped tears from their eyes with the back of their hands, and Hall blew his nose into his hand. They took the opportunity to rub their bare, smarting bottoms, showing their genitals.

Mr Buckmaster's eyes widened as he looked at Wilde's shaved nether regions.

"Are you shaved because that is what you want, or are you acting under instructions, Wilde?" he asked.

Wilde's face blushed crimson. "I guess it's a lifestyle choice, Sir," he replied.

He noticed that Hall was struggling to take his punishment, even though his hardening cock might tell otherwise. "Are you all right Hall?" he asked. Hall just nodded.

"Hall is upset about what happened last night Sir," Wilde said.

"Why are you upset, Hall?" Mr Buckmaster asked.

"Um, just stuff about last night Sir," Hall said evasively.

"I can't help you, Hall, if you won't tell me what is bothering you," Mr Buckmaster said.

"I am ok, Sir," Hall replied.

"Very well, have it your way. Both of you – bend over again for another six," he said.

The boys bent over their desks again and pushed their bare bottoms into position.

Mr Buckmaster gave Hall another six licks of the strap, but he laid them on lightly. Hall still cried out as he responded to each lick, his penis lolling left and right, his cockhead exposed.

"Remain where you are, Hall," Mr Buckmaster said as he proceeded to give Wilde six full-force licks of his strap. Wilde gasped and cried out as he took his punishment.

Mr Buckmaster rubbed his hand over Wilde's hairless bottom, slowly massaging each of his well-rounded, bruised orbs.

"Oh Sir, I am enjoying that, but is it permissible for you to touch my bare bottom?" Wilde asked cheekily.

"Don't be impertinent, boy," Mr Buckmaster snapped. "I can see you train a lot."

"Yes, Sir. I like to keep it firm and hard."

The punishment complete, Mr Buckmaster made both lads face the wall with their hands on top of their heads. Their bare, well-strapped bottoms were badly bruised and mooned provocatively. And they moved and massaged them, just to tease their punisher, who began to sweat, fighting the urge to touch and caress them.

...

Dillon was sleeping off the big night out that he had enjoyed with his three rugby friends. Davenport woke him.

"Wake up, Dillon. You are to report to Mr Seeking as soon as possible," he said as he shook him.

"Go away and let me die in peace," Dillon moaned.

Davenport shrugged his shoulders and tipped his bed over, depositing Dillon onto the floor. Dillon lay naked among his discarded clothes and bedding. He quickly covered his impressive morning woody with a bedsheet.

The strong odour of his musk pervaded the room.

"Fuck off Davenport," he said.

"Mr Seeking said as soon as possible. Now get yourself cleaned up and put your uniform on. If you tell me to *fuck off* again, I will cane you," Davenport threatened.

Davenport escorted a hung-over Dillon to the security gate. "My office, Dillon," Mr Seeking said.

Reg Seeking and Zac Dillon went back a long way, they had served in the army together where Mr Seeking had been his platoon sergeant.

"What's this about, Reg?" Dillon asked.

"This is a disciplinary matter, so you will address me as Sir," Mr Seeking said.

"What?" Dillon asked incredulously.

"Why didn't you come back with Hall and Wilde last night?" he asked.

"Well, I met some lads I know from St Andrew's rugby, and we decided to make a night of it," Dillon replied.

"Sir," Mr Seeking reminded him.

"Sir," Dillon said.

"And you left Hall and Wilde in the Burger Treat restaurant," Mr Seeking said.

"Yes, I did Sir. I told them that I was going to join my St Andrews friends and that they were to get their arses back to the Academy," Dillon said.

Mr Seeking told Dillon that they hadn't returned to the Academy and that they had been arrested by the Banks police in the early hours of the morning for vagrancy.

"What? Where are they now?" Dillon asked.

"They are being dealt with by Mr Buckmaster as we speak," Mr Seeking said.

Dillon put his head in his hands and said, "Oh no, it's all my fault."

Mr Seeking looked at Dillon and said, "You took those two boys out. They were looking to you for leadership, they trusted you and you have let them down, Dillon."

Dillon could offer no excuse for his behaviour. "Yes Sir. No excuse Sir," he said.

"Report to Mr Buckmaster and explain yourself," Dillon, Mr Seeking said.

"Yes Sir," Dillon replied.

Dillon knocked once on the classroom door and then entered the room. Mr Buckmaster was sitting at his desk recording the punishment he had awarded the lads on the police charge sheets. Hall and Wilde were standing facing the wall their bare backsides had a red hue and were covered with black and blue bruises attesting to their recent strapping. He felt a pang of guilt as he saw that they had their arms around each other's shoulders, comforting each other.

Mr Buckmaster looked up and said, "Ah Dillon, come in. you have some explaining to do."

"Yes, Sir. This was all my fault," he said.

Wilde and Hall turned to face him, the humiliation that he had heaped on them the night before was fresh in their memories.

"It's a bit late for that Dillon," Wilde said.

"I fucking hate you Dillon," Hall hissed.

"That's enough, both of you!" Mr Buckmaster shouted. "I will speak to you later about your language, Hall," he added. He then told them to get dressed and leave.

The lads got dressed, and as a surreptitious act of defiance, they picked up each other's underpants. They carefully pulled them and their trousers over their smarting bottoms.

Mr Buckmaster gave Hall the police charge sheets that he had completed and told him to give them to Mr Seeking. "They have to be returned to the court," he said.

"Yes, Sir," Hall said.

"Come here Dillon. Stand to attention in front of my desk," Mr Buckmaster said.

Dillon decided to confess everything to his form master, to hold nothing back and to throw himself upon his mercy.

"Why did you leave Hall and Wilde alone in town last night?" Mr Buckmaster asked.

Red-faced, Dillon admitted that he had gone to Suzie's bar with three friends from the St Andrew's rugby.

"Did the temptation to behave like a lad get too much for you?" Mr Buckmaster asked.

"Yes, but I didn't want them to think that Academy lads were a bunch of wimps, Sir," Dillon said.

Mr Buckmaster told him that it was a pathetic excuse and that obeying the headmaster's edict was the manly thing to do. He reminded Dillon that this was the second time that he had defied Academy regulations and visited Suzie's bar.

Dillon hung his head and said, "Yes, Sir."

"How did you get back to the Academy?" Mr Buckmaster asked.

"The lads gave me a lift and I climbed over the back fence, Sir," he admitted.

"To avoid being put on report for being late back,"

"Yes Sir."

Mr. Buckmaster shook his head gravely. "Dillon, you've managed to alienate your friends, disobey the Headmaster's orders for the second time, and violate Academy discipline. Can you give me a reason you shouldn't be expelled?" he asked.

"I'm sorry, Sir. I know I've screwed up. If you give me another chance, I promise that I will make it right with my friends Hall and Wilde, and with you and the Academy, Sir," Dillon pleaded.

Mr. Buckmaster contemplated Dillon's future. While he understood that young men like Dillon needed to sow their wild oats, he also knew that there had to be consequences for his misbehaviour. He decided to offer Dillon another opportunity.

"Academy discipline in the form of restrictions, the cane and strap will deal with your infractions, Dillon. But you also have a lot of fence-mending to do with your friends, and I can't help you with that," Mr Buckmaster said.

"Yes Sir. I understand, thank you, Sir," Dillon said.

Mr Buckmaster gave him his punishment. "You are to receive twelve strokes of the cane followed by six licks of the strap, all on your bare bottom. You are also grounded for the rest of the semester. This is going to sting Dillon," he said.

"Yes, Sir. Thank you, Sir," Dillon gulped, as he started to strip under Mr Buckmaster hard stare.

...

Their butts smarting, Hall and Wilde reported to the security gate and delivered their completed charge sheets to Mr Seeking.

Mr Seeking wanted the lads to settle their differences, he spoke to them about their behaviour the night before. "I warned you, boys, to behave yourselves. You should have done what Dillon told you to do and returned to the Academy," he said.

But Hall was obdurate. "Why should we listen to a person who walked out on us," he argued.

He advised them to work together, admit that there was fault on both sides and to forgive.

"Perhaps, but only after he has eaten lots of humble pie, Sir," Hall replied.

Mt Seeking shook his head. Hall could be very stubborn sometimes.

On their way back to their dorm, the boys went past Mr Buckmaster's classroom to see how Dillon was faring. They peered through a window and watched as Mr Buckmaster's strap rose and fell across his muscular, red, naked orbs. He hollered loudly, naked and sweated, as each lick bit deeply into his freshly caned bottom, his penis hard as it had never been – such an erotic sight. They both grinned. It was good to see Dillon getting what was coming to him, even though they knew that at least a part of him was enjoying all that.

They moved on. Oska asked, "Can I sleep in your room tonight, Eugene?"

"Of course," Eugene said. "I was hoping that you would ask. We can have some fun. Are you... excited by what you saw?"

"Oh... terribly," Oska answered, showing the bulge in his pants.

Eugene smiled. "I will try to help you with that."

The end.

MELISSA TRUMP

Look at the books in the same series:

https://www.amazon.com/dp/B0CWZ64WYN?binding=kindle_edition&ref=dbs_dp_rwt_sb_pc_tkin

Or take a look at the other series of the author:

Exciting erotica fiction in various historical settings with slaves:

https://www.amazon.com/dp/B0CR1R3S9W?binding=kindle_edition&ref=dbs_dp_rwt_sb_pc_tkin

Sex Education at Sea (the story of a young mariner and slave, traveling around the whole world in the '500)

https://www.amazon.com/dp/B0CTX5JZ1S?binding=kindle_edition&ref=dbs_dp_rwt_sb_pc_tkin

Wild Stories (A thirty year-old nascar driver with his young assistant, or a spanking communist master, you choose!)

https://www.amazon.com/dp/B0CR73TZ69?binding=kindle_edition&ref=dbs_dp_rwt_sb_pc_tkin

Sex Education Camp (role play for 18 and 19 year olds people in a relaxing summer camp)

https://www.amazon.com/dp/B0CKZBNNMQ?binding=kindle_edition&ref=dbs_dp_rwt_sb_pc_tkin

Strip boy Strip (stories about stripping and watching youths undressing)

https://www.amazon.com/dp/B0CVLJT7XK?binding=kindle_edition&ref=dbs_dp_rwt_sb_pc_tkin

Young Gladiators (mainly slaves fighting nude for personal glory or survival)

https://www.amazon.com/dp/B0CTHQCRZH?binding=kindle_edition&ref=dbs_dp_rwt_sb_pc_tkin

Made in United States
Troutdale, OR
02/02/2026